Fer my posse:
Rachel, Samuel,
and Matthew

Library of Congress
Cataloging-in-Publication Data
McClements, George.
Ridin' dinos with Buck Bronco/
George McClements.
p. cm.
Summary: Buck Bronco teaches
how to care for and ride
a variety of strange dinosaurs.
[1. Dinosaurs—Fiction.
2. Cowboys—Fiction.
3. Humorous stories.] I. Title.
II. Title: Ridin' dinos with Buck Bronco.
PZ7.M1325Ri 2007
[E]—dc22   2006006175
ISBN 978-0-15-205989-7

First edition

A C E G H F D B

Manufactured in China

The illustrations in this book
were created using mixed-media collage.
The display type was set in Rootin' Tootin'.
The text type was set in Zalderdash.
Color separations by Bright Arts Ltd., Hong Kong
Manufactured by South China Printing Company, Ltd., Chin
Production supervision by Christine Witnik
Designed by Lauren Rille

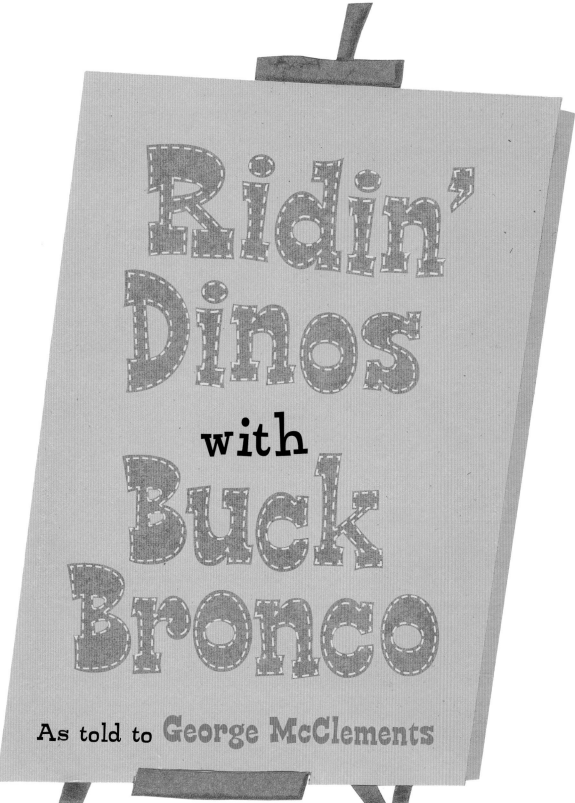

Ridin' Dinos

with

Buck Bronco

As told to George McClements

Ship to:
HARCOURT, INC.
Orlando   Austin
New York
San Diego
Toronto
London

Howdy, kids! The name is

onco,

and I'm here to teach y'all everything
you need to know 'bout ridin' dinosaurs,
includin' how I met these curious critters.

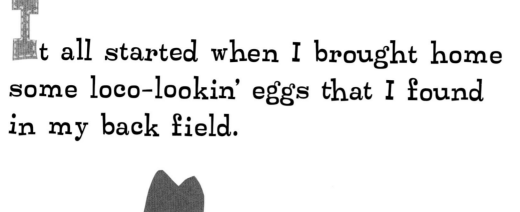

It all started when I brought home
some loco-lookin' eggs that I found
in my back field.

I was surely surprised
when they began to hatch.

I had to do some quick-time learnin'.

And today I'm called
a leadin' authority on dinosaurs.

Now let's stop all
this tongue waggin'
and git to ridin'!

Choosin' Yer Mount

First, you'll need to pick out a dino from my Mesozoic Ranch. I have three different stables to choose from.

TRIASSIC

Biped=2 legs

You'll have to decide between the speed of a biped or the comfort of a quadruped.

Quadruped=4 legs

You vegetarians out there may want to choose an herbivore over a steak-chompin' carnivore.

Dinosaurs come in
so many shapes and sizes,
I'm sure you'll find one
to match yer personality.

Saddlin' Yer Dino

Next, unless ya got glue in yer britches,
we'll need to tack up!

Take a look at what we got:

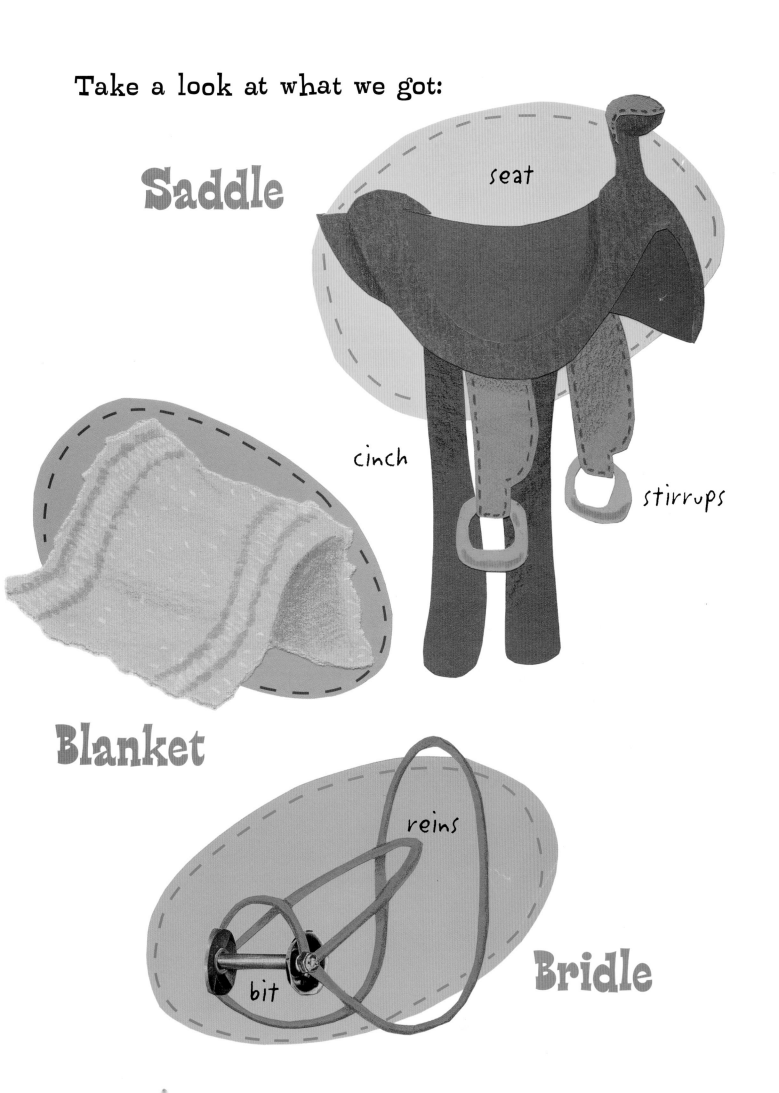

Saddle

seat

cinch

stirrups

Blanket

reins

bit

Bridle

A little creativity helps with the big boys.

Diplodocus = 88 feet long

I like to use somethin' called the polecat hop to git into my saddle.

First, you line up yer seat...

then you kick up some dust...

grab some air...

...and two somersaults later, yer sittin' pretty.

A kentrosaurus may present some special problems, so I suggest usin' a ladder.

Now that we're strapped in, let's git movin'! Luckily, I got these handy talkin' boards to help us along.

After the Ride

It's not all about doin' fancy tricks and showboat jumps. We have to take care of our prehistoric pals.

Yer dinosaur will be powerful thirsty after all that runnin' around. So make certain he gits his fill of water.

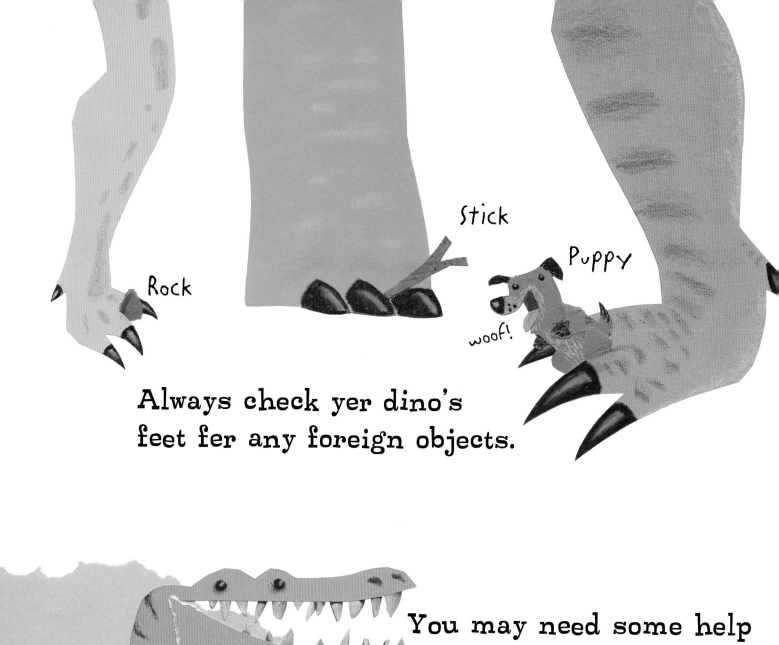

Always check yer dino's feet fer any foreign objects.

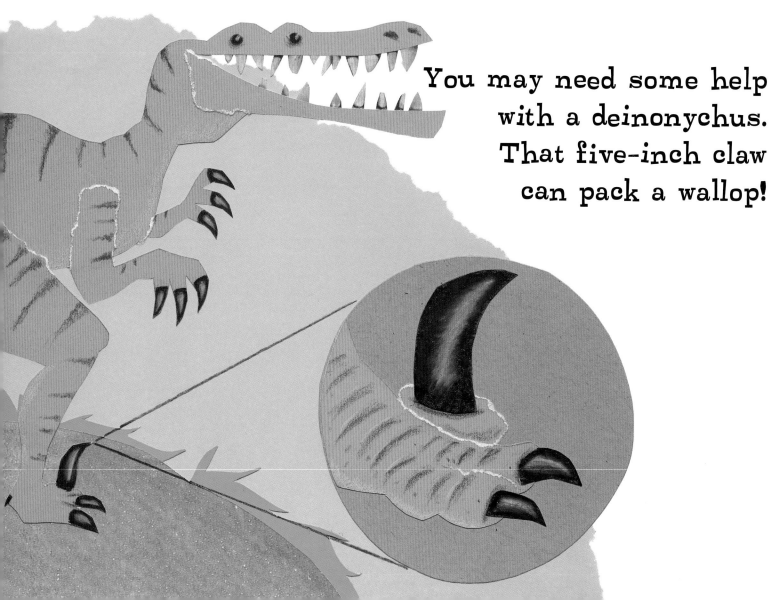

You may need some help with a deinonychus. That five-inch claw can pack a wallop!

These critters can sure work up an appetite.
Here's a few suggestions fer suppertime:

Herbivores

leaves

nuts and berries

low-lying shrubs

Carnivores

meat

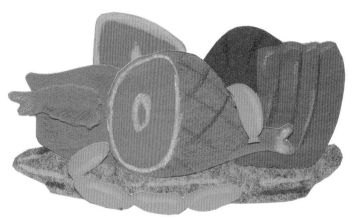

meat

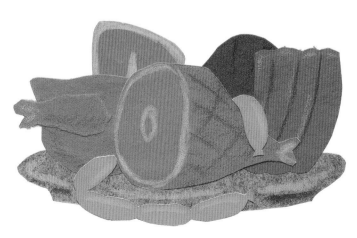

meat

At the End of the Day

Compsognathus=40 inches

Size 12 ½

Don't forget to give yer dino a comfy place to bed down.

I find it best to let the big guys
pick their own spots.

Spinosaurus=40 feet

Y'all are probably wonderin' why I'm sharin' my dino secrets. The truth be told, I was hopin' y'all could help me out.

Now that yer dinosaur experts...

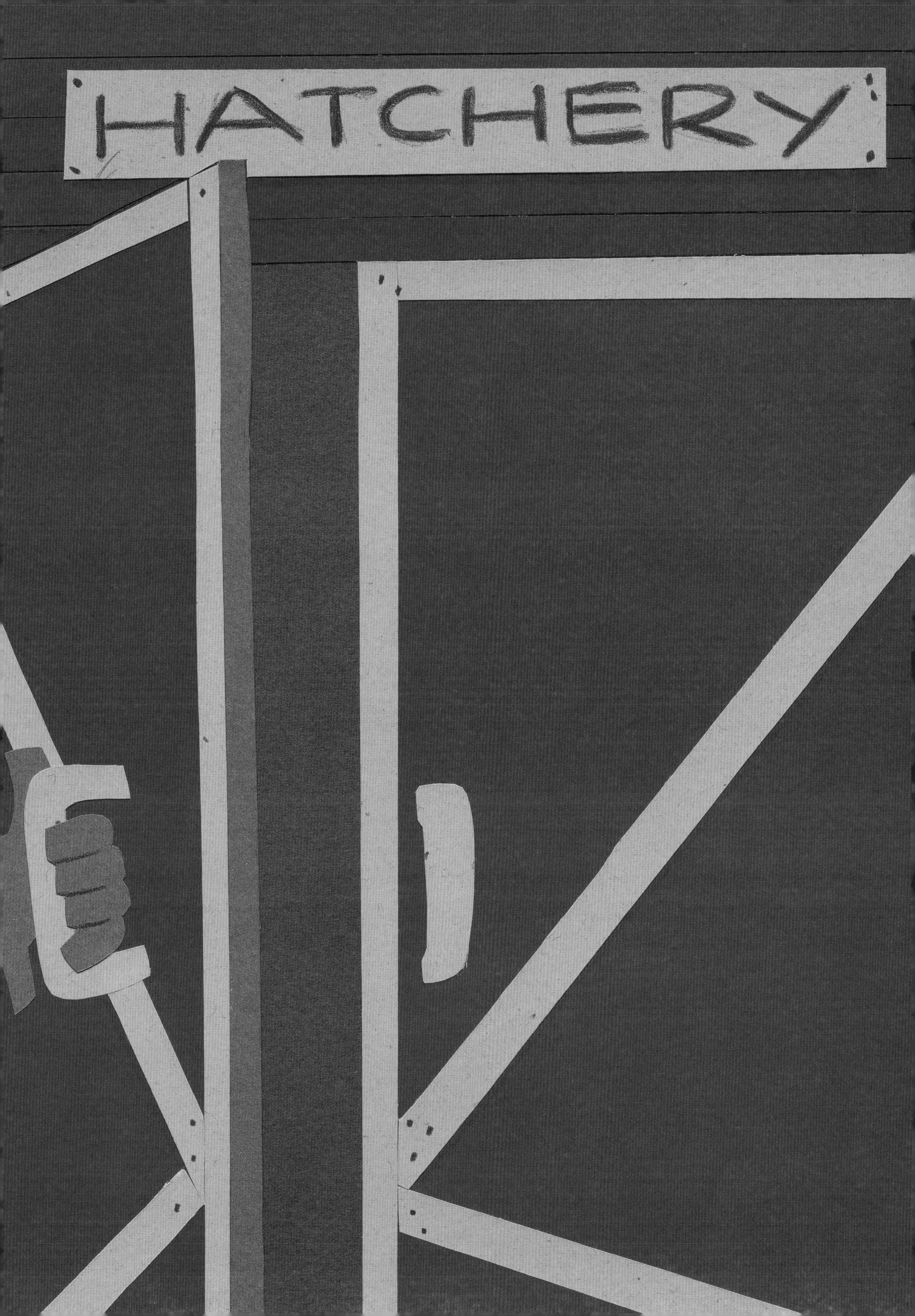
HATCHERY

Would you mind if
I sent you a couple
of eggs?